Adapted by Lisa Ann Marsoli
Based on the episode written by Ashley Mendoza
Illustrated by Loter, Inc.

ABDOPUBLISHING.COM

Reinforced library bound edition published in 2019 by Spotlight, a division of ABDO, PO Box 398166, Minneapolis, Minnesota 55439. Spotlight produces high-quality reinforced library bound editions for schools and libraries. Published by agreement with Disney Press, an imprint of Disney Book Group.

Printed in the United States of America, North Mankato, Minnesota.
042018   092018

Di**SNEP** PRESS
New York • Los Angeles

THIS BOOK CONTAINS
RECYCLED MATERIALS

Library of Congress Control Number: 2017961283

Publisher's Cataloging in Publication Data

Names: Marsoli, Lisa Ann, author. | Mendoza, Ashley, author. | Loter, Inc., illustrator.
Title: Mickey Mouse Clubhouse: Minnie-rella / by Lisa Ann Marsoli and Ashley Mendoza; illustrated by Loter, Inc.
Description: Minneapolis, MN : Spotlight, 2019 | Series: World of reading level 1
Summary: Minnie falls asleep while doing chores and dreams that she becomes Minnierella.
Identifiers: ISBN 9781532141911 (lib. bdg.)
Subjects: LCSH: Mickey Mouse Clubhouse (Television program)--Juvenile fiction. | Mouse, Minnie (Fictitious character)--Juvenile fiction. | Dreams--Juvenile fiction. | Cinderella (Tale)--Juvenile fiction. | Readers (Primary)---Juvenile fiction.
Classification: DDC [E]--dc23

Spotlight
A Division of ABDO
abdopublishing.com

Mickey wants to surprise Minnie.
He needs to keep Minnie busy.
"Can you take care of my frog?"
Goofy asks.

"And sweep the floor?" Daisy adds.
"And wash my rubber duckies?"
says Donald.

"I have a lot to do," says Minnie.
First she washes the rubber duckies.

Next she fixes Pluto's bear.
"I'm so tired," says Minnie.
Soon she is asleep!

"Minnie-rella!" a voice calls.
"I'm your fairy godmother! It's time
to get ready for Prince Mickey's ball!"
Minnie-rella has too much to do.

The Fairy Godmother will help.
She waves her wand.
Oops! Flowers grow out of the floor!
"Oh, Quoodles," she calls.

Quoodles brings a pillow, a hippo,
a ribbon, and the mystery tool.
They will save the tools for later.

The Handy Helpers help clean.
"Now you can go to Prince Mickey's ball,"
the Fairy Godmother says.

"I need a dress," says Minnie-rella.
"Here," the Fairy Godmother says.
Oh, no! The dress is in pieces!
"Oops!" says the Fairy Godmother.

The Fairy Godmother whistles.
Some little friends come to help.
Soon Minnie-rella has a lovely dress.

Now Minnie-rella needs a new bow.
"Hmmm," says the Fairy Godmother.
"Which tool can we use?"
"The ribbon!" says Minnie-rella.

The Fairy Godmother looks down.
"Your shoes won't do at all!" she cries.

She waves her
wand once.

"Oops!"

She tries again.

"Oops!"

"Once more," says
the Fairy Godmother.

"That's it!"

"You're ready!" says the Fairy Godmother.
"How will I get there?" asks Minnie-rella.
They go to Goofy's garden.

The Fairy Godmother asks for a pumpkin.
"I don't have any pumpkins," Goofy says.
"But I've got a big tomato."

The tomato turns into a carriage.
Goofy turns into a coachman!
"Be home before midnight!"
says the Fairy Godmother.

On the way to the ball, the carriage
gets stuck in a hole!
Minnie-rella calls Quoodles.
Which tool can help?

Maybe the hippo can push the
carriage out of the hole!
The hippo taps the carriage.
Away it goes!

Soon Minnie-rella and Goofy come
to the castle gate.
"It takes three diamonds to unlock
the gate," Pete says.

20

Quoodles brings the mystery tool.
It is a bracelet with three diamonds.
The three diamonds unlock the gate.
Minnie-rella can go to the ball!

Minnie-rella runs to the ball.
She dances with Prince Mickey.
Prince Mickey has found his princess!

Soon it is midnight.

"I have to go!" cries Minnie-rella.

"Wait! I don't know your name,"
Prince Mickey calls.

"How will I find her?" he asks.
Pluto sees the glass slipper.
Prince Mickey must find the one
who fits the glass slipper.

Prince Mickey begins his search.
Goofy tries on the glass slipper.
It does not fit.

The slipper is going to break!
Quoodles brings the pillow.
Prince Mickey catches the slipper!

Goofy takes him to see Minnie-rella.
The glass slipper fits!

The prince and princess will live
happily ever after!

"Wake up, Minnie!" call her friends.
Mickey gives her a present.
"I dreamed of shoes like these!"
Minnie says. "Thank you!"

"You look like a princess,"
says Mickey.
"You'll always be my prince!"
Minnie says.

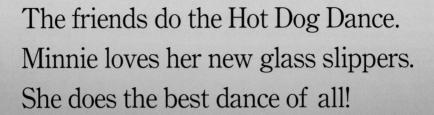

The friends do the Hot Dog Dance.
Minnie loves her new glass slippers.
She does the best dance of all!